HARD TIME

ALEX LAYBOURNE

SEVERED PRESS
Hobart Tasmania

HARD TIME

Copyright © 2015 by Alex Laybourne
Copyright © 2015 by Severed Press

www.severedpress.com

This novel is a work of fiction. Names, characters, places and incidents are the product of the author's imagination, or are used fictitiously.
Any resemblance to actual events, locales or persons, living or dead, is purely coincidental.

ISBN: 978-1-925342-42-0

CHAPTER 1 – TIME SERVED

The door to the warden's office flew open. Looking up from his desk Randolph Walker looked surprised. People knew better than to interrupt him. Jumping to his feet he floundered, springing up from behind his desk as his trousers fell around his ankles. His face was red from exertion, and the shade only deepened with his embarrassment.

The young prison guard stood with bulging eyes as the young female inmate got out from under the desk, wiping her mouth as she walked out of the room. She winked at the young guard.

"Any time you want it, just ask." She ran her hand down his arm and pinched his behind as she walked away.

"What is the meaning of this?" The warden roared, pulling the young guards attention back to the office.

The warden had re-fastened his trousers and was striding from behind his desk, intent on making the young man suffer for embarrassing him.

"I'm sorry sir, but... but... Captain Jones said I needed to come to you right away." The boy stammered, flustered by the charging warden and the news which he had yet to explain.

"What's your name, boy?" The warden asked. He was close enough for the young guard to feel the heat of the man's rage radiating from him.

"We've got a parolee, sir." The man stammered, intent on delivering his news and getting out of the way.

The warden looked at the man and suddenly his face broke. A laugh escaped his lips, which turned upwards into a smile. It was an expression that made the young man even more nervous.

"A parolee. Oh of course, that makes perfect sense. How long have you worked in this prison... whatever your name is?" The warden's eyes bored holes into the young man's chest.

"Peter Malone, sir. I've been working here almost six months, sir." Peter answered sheepishly. At nineteen years old, he was young to be on the staff at Kruger Correctional. He had joined the Marines at the age of eighteen, and his placement at Kruger had been at his own request.

"Well, Mr. Malone. In those six months, how many people have you seen paroled?" The warden's voice was patronizing, as if he was talking to a small child.

Peter swallowed hard. Uncomfortable with the direction the conversation was going. "Several sir, from the light offender's wing." Peter felt the sweat run down his back. His heart was racing.

"Well then, pray tell. What was so important about this parolee that you felt it wise to come barging into my office without so much as a courteous knock?" There was a calm in the warden's voice that made Peter shiver. He knew he needed to be careful with his response, for there was a chance he would not get the chance to finish delivering his news before the warden finished him off.

"Well, this one isn't a light offender, sir. This one is from … there." He felt a rush of adrenaline surge through him at the mere mention of the high level offenders' institution.

The warden froze for a second. The wind had been taken from his sails. "Ok. I don't know why Captain Jones sent you to me. He knows full well how to deal with such a situation. I take it this is your first time. It's a simple process, just paperwork really. Moving files to archive, and clearing out the lockers, and stuff." The warden was still annoyed, but the edge of his rage had fallen away.

"No sir." Peter interrupted, silently flinching at the sudden gasp the Warden took at being interrupted. He needed to act fast. "It's not like that, sir. This one is… well, it looks like he is still alive." Peter's eyes stung from the sweat that leaked into them, but he stood tall before his boss.

The warden's face changed. His mouth fell open and his eyes widened in disbelief. "It's not possible. It's a false reading. We get them from time to time." He moved away from Peter and back to his desk. "Come here, we will check the logs." The interruption was forgotten.

"Captain Jones already checked sir. There are clear signs of life and movement. He even checked the second level calculations and can see heart rate and blood pressure readings throughout. They are all consistent with this inmate still being alive." Peter swallowed hard. Delivering the news about a man's life should not have been this hard, yet he found himself growing more nervous with every bit of evidence he offered.

"That's not possible." The warden gasped, a sense of urgency creeping into his voice. "Take me to Captain Jones, now," he ordered, leaving his office at a pace close to a run. Peter remained where was for a few moments, taken aback by everything he had seen happen. "Are you coming rookie?" The warden's voice called from the corridor.

Kruger Correctional was the largest penitentiary on the West Coast and played home to four different units all independently contained and centrally controlled in one large complex that covered an area larger than some small countries. The warden's office was located in the same area as the low level and juvenile corrections. Low level offenders were typically those jailed for repetitive violations of simple offenses. Drunk and disorderly or driving while under the influence being the more common items, although parking fines was a close third.

Leaving the complex, the warden got into the waiting car and beckoned Peter to join him. "Come on, we don't have all day," he said hurried. "Take us to Zone One," he instructed the driver. "And please call ahead and tell Captain Jones that I expect him to be waiting for me when I arrive, preferably with some answers." Without waiting for a response, the warden closed the partition that separated passenger from driver, and turned his attention to Peter.

"So tell me, Mr. Malone. What was it that made you want to come here so earnestly?" He looked at Peter with an interested gaze. His face was stern and impossible to read.

Peter thought about the answer. It came easily to the forefront of his mind, but putting words to it, giving it life, was a different matter entirely.

"Out with it man. I highly doubt it was for the prospect of blowjobs from Molly Harriot." The warden barked a laugh at his own joke, the embarrassment of their initial meeting now forgotten. "Not that I would blame you. Out of all of them, she has the best mouth." He winked at Peter. "Gotta enjoy the perks while they last." He smiled again and pulled out his cell.

"Actually sir, it was because of my mother. I always wanted to join the military, but she never wanted me going overseas. I was her only child and she raised me alone. This was a compromise I guess." Peter lied.

"Oh, and I was expecting it to be because your father was imprisoned here for so many years." The warden looked at Peter and nodded at him with a self-satisfactory smirk on his face as he read the young man's expression.

"How did you…" Peter began

"How did I know? Just because you change your name it doesn't mean that you hide your past." The warden winked at Peter. "Listen, I like you kid. I was the one who approved your application when nobody else thought you could do it. I know the truth about everything around here, so don't let anything people say fool you. And don't ever lie to me again. I have big plans for you, alright." The warden leaned over and patted Peter on the knee. "Lighten up kid. So your dad was a mass murderer. It doesn't mean you will be too." The warden scowled. "Unless you have some dark secret?" With a seriousness that could only be taken as an attempt at humour.

"No sir, I'm not. I never really knew my Dad, and I thought being here, I might, learn a little bit about it."

The warden didn't have time to offer an answer, for their car came to a stop and a few moments later the door was opened for them. Climbing out, they stared at the building which, for all intents and purposes looked no more like a maximum security prison wing than it did a public swimming pool.

The building was plain and unassuming. It looked like, and in a previous life had been, a large stately home. Owned by a rich family with a heritage going back many years. Their fortune lost or squandered to the ravages of time. The building had been the first acquisition of the Kruger Correctional complex. Back then it had started off as a research laboratory specializing in the analysis of the criminal mind. The problem with criminal activity was growing, and as the twenty-first century neared its midpoint, it was decided that alternative methods were required in order to both contain and control the countries more troublesome and violent inmates.

Peter walked beside the warden, although he was ready to take the customary, and respectful step back should the need arise. They rang the intercom on the door and a camera immediately turned towards them. A radio mounted on the gate cracked with static and the voice of one of the guards in the house came through.

"It's Warden Rose. Open up, I'm here to see Captain Jones." The warden had not even finished talking and the electronic lock on the door clicked open.

Captain Jones was waiting for them. "Thank you for coming to see me warden." He marched towards the pair as they entered the house and shook he warden's hand. "That's all for now Malone. Report back to your station and resume your normal duties." The captain ordered. He was an old school military man, from a military bloodline. He dressed in full military attire every day, and never moved at a pace that varied above or below that of a march.

"No, that's fine. I want young Peter here to be involved. It is his parolee and I feel he is ready for the challenge." The warden contradicted the order, and left Peter frozen in mid departure.

"With all due respect warden, he is a rookie…" Captain Jones made no attempt to hide his disapproval.

"With all due respect captain, I do not give a flying shit about him being a rookie. He is seeing this through and I will not have my decisions questioned, are we clear?" The warden was not angry, his voice was calm and flat, but the words and his facial expression spoke volumes. Captain Jones took one look and stood down.

"Yes sir, warden," he answered, shooting a glare towards Peter who was more confused than ever. "Let me take you to the monitoring station, show you what we have learned thus far." Jones spoke as they walked away.

"Is there any chance that it was a false reading?" The warden asked as they moved through the house.

"No sir. This man is alive. We have tripled checked the numbers." Jones didn't look at them as he talked, but kept moving, up the stairs to the third floor of the house.

The control room was a large space that occupied most of the renovated floor. Computer terminals were spread around the room, with a mix of civilian workers and military personnel sitting behind them. The computers were divided into five groups, and each one was responsible for a different offender type.

Peter had only left the room a short time before, but the buzz of activity in it had increased dramatically. Everybody froze when the warden arrived. All eyes moved to him. He was in charge, his rank high above that of any military man in the complex.

"Alright people, there's nothing to see here. Back to work," he ordered, and smiled as everybody obeyed his command.

"Captain Jones, show me the statistics on the prisoner." He was all business.

"Yes sir." Captain Jones answered, leading both the warden and Peter through the room to the desk area where Peter had been stationed. "The initial reports were received here, but we also have it linked to the main computer in the office. We can look there if you would rather." Jones offered.

"No, here will be fine." The warden was already sitting behind the machine, his hands moving over the keyboard at speed.

Data and recorded readings appeared all over the screen, as the warden scanned through the activity logs, blood pressure history and all of the vital sign recordings dating back as far back as the man's original incarceration.

"Tell me Captain Jones. What did this man do?" The warden sat back in the desk chair, his hands clasped on his chest, fingers interlocked.

"He shot and killed a man." Captain Jones answered,

"In cold blood?" The warden was testing Jones. Peter knew this from their conversation in the car; the way the warden knew about his father.

"Yes sir. He shot and killed the man who was driving the car that killed his own wife and child." To Captain Jones a murder was a murder, regardless of circumstance. The only ones that did not count were those of his men and the lives they had claimed over the years on their tours of duty."

The warden took a long, slow breath. "How long has he been inside?" The warden spoke aloud as he ran through the case file on the computer screen.

"He has been inside for twelve years, sir. He was one of the year one entrants, sir." Captain Jones answered again, although it was clear to see from his face that he was growing rather tired of the question and answer game.

"This data does look rather conclusive. We always knew this day would come Captain. Assemble your men. We have a man who has served his time and has earned his release." The warden looked from the Captain to the computer screen. His face was pensive.

Captain Jones saluted the warden and dismissed himself in true military fashion. Peter moved to follow but the warden called him back. "Peter, a moment of your time, please." His voice was soft, almost a whisper.

"Yes, warden?" Peter turned.

"I want you to go in with the extraction team. It will be a good experience for you." Peter felt a strange rush of emotion surge through him. The task itself was a great honour, and for someone as young as he was, it was a sign of great trust and confidence. At the same time however, Peter knew the sort of people that waited for him in the maximum security ward.

"Thank you, sir." Peter was starting to sweat.

"I trust you Peter, and I have a good feeling about you. My gut is never wrong." He added the second sentence as justification given their short time in each other's company. "I also need you to do something for me."

"Yes, sir. Anything you need." Peter said. He was young but not stupid. He knew where he stood, and that eagerness counted for a lot in his future.

"I need you to keep an eye on Captain Jones. I am concerned about him. He is not the young man he was. Where you are going, it is no walk in the park. There are more dangers there than you could imagine." The warden's words carried a heavy impact, and Peter nodded, not needing any more explanation, the same way no more response was required from him in order for the warden to know his point had been understood.

CHAPTER 2 — THE LOST WORLD

Thirty minutes later the team were assembled in the building's basement. There were eight men including Peter, who would be going in for the extraction. They were heavily armed and also had a large container filled with food and supplies which was waiting for them at the transport zone.

"Gentlemen," The warden began, standing before the assembled men like a brave and bold leader. "I want this extraction to go just the way we have always run it in practice. This is a first for us, and you can be assured that your return will be greeted by a media storm. There are spa uniforms in the supply crate for you all. Please put them on as you prepare to return home, we need you looking your best for the cameras." The warden paced up and down as he spoke. The nonchalant way he referred to the task that lay before them was anything but comforting.

"Jackass." Peter heard someone whisper from behind them.

"Got no idea." The whispered response came. Peter wanted to turn around, to ask them what it was really like out there. But he didn't, he couldn't move.

With his speech over, the warden moved to one side and Captain Jones stepped forward, turning to face the group. He took his time, looking at each man in turn. His gaze seemed to linger on Peter more than anybody else, but Peter was unfazed.

"This is not your every day stroll in the park ladies. We are going into some hostile territory. None of us have been there before. The people we are going to face have been out there a long time. They were no angels when they were here, you can bet your ass they aren't angels now either. We are going inside in two teams of four. James, Michaels, Peart and Wilson, you guys are going to follow us through. Set up camp. I will take Stevens, Moose and the rookie here, and we will sweep the area. Make sure it's all clear. We're not playing games here, so if we shoot, we shoot to kill. Got it?" His eyes once again focused on Peter, and the expression amplified the contempt his words had held when addressing him.

"Yes, sir." The group responded as one.

Each team got into the car that was waiting for them and they headed out of the basement level carpark and across the facility a short way to the transport centre. It was not until the shadow of the centre loomed over him that Peter began to feel nervous. Even having an M-16 slung over his shoulder did little to improve his confidence. He hid it well however.

Inside the transport centre there was a buzz of activity. The engineers in command were not used to sending such large numbers. Since the flow of incoming prisoners was so steady, the warden had agreed to transport people as and when they arrived, rather than keep them in containment for no reason.

News of their departure had spread fast, for the machines were already fired up by the time they arrived.

"Remember gentlemen, the terrain we are going to is familiar to the inmates. We need to watch our backs, move swiftly but with caution. Who knows what sort of traps they have set for us in there." Captain Jones gave his final speech as he stood on the transport pod. Peter was beside him. They looked at one another. "You ready rookie?" There was a smile on the Captain's face. The jokes were over. They were a team now. Their lives were interlinked in a way that could never be broken. Whatever the Captain or the others felt, Peter was one of them now, and they would begrudgingly treat him as such.

"Yes, sir." Peter answered. He meant it too. His nerves had fallen away the moment he stood on his pod.

"Gentlemen, I shall see you on the battlefield." Captain Jones spoke, as the group saluted the room.

Everything dissolved in an instant. The pod, the floor, the gathered crowd; everything vanished, and all that was left, was black. A strange warm blackness. Peter's knees felt week and his head swam with an intoxicated sensation. His stomach turned and as a wave of nausea passed through him, the world came back into focus.

Green, he was surrounded by green. Trees and plants were all around him, and loomed as tall as anything he had ever seen. Behind him some animal gave a roar. Spinning around, gripping his M-16 with both hands, he looked for the others. He saw them all moving through the trees, looking for a place to rendezvous and plan their search of the area.

Protocol dictated that the second group would come through fifteen minutes after the first, and so they were on their own until then.

"Rookie, over here." Captain Jones called through the trees. Peter turned his body and looked. He saw the captain and the space the others were moving to.

"What is this place?" Stevens asked, looked at the towering vegetation. "I've never seen a place like it."

"It doesn't matter. We need to clear the area and make way for the second group. I want to be in an out of this place faster than a greased up weasel down a hole. Now let's move," Jones answered, pointing in the direction they should head.

The clearing they had found was not large enough to serve as a base for them all, and the idea of a split camp was no a favourable option. Moving as fast as they could the four soldiers covered the ground in search of a better location. The vegetation was thick, and the temperature beneath the trees was extraordinary.

Peter was already soaked with sweat after having moved fifty feet from where they had touched down. Looking around him, he saw that the others had been swallowed by the trees. Wiping his brow, he looked at his watch. They had twelve minutes before the other team arrived, and when they did, they would be sent to the location of the GPS tracker Jones carried with him.

Something rustled in the trees to his left. Peter raised his weapon, finger curling around the trigger. He wasn't sure what to expect. The rustling moved all around him. Whatever it was, it was fast, and it felt to Peter as if he were being stalked.

Squinting his eyes, Peter peered at the spot where the rustling seemed to have stopped. He could make out a shape, but his eyes could not distinguish it. The jungle swallowed everything after a few feet; obscuring it in total shadow.

The scream made him jump. The burst of gunfire made him run. Charging back the way he had come, Peter headed in the direction from which he thought the shots had originated. Hurtling a large root that was raised a good three inches from the ground, Peter ran into the clearing. There was no sign of any struggle. Jones arrived a few moments later, and Moose reached them from the right seconds later.

"Where's Stevens?" Jones asked, looking at both of them. His face a deep shade of red thanks to the heat.

"He went that way." Peter pointed to a gap in the trees. He had noticed it because of the strange way the first two trees that rose above Steven's path were both badly damaged, with deep gouges carved into their trunks.

"Come with me. Remember, shoot to kill." Jones ordered, moving into the trees. He kept his body down; a low centre of gravity.

Peter followed his captain, while Moose brought up the rear. The jungle seemed to open up for them as they moved after Stevens. There were signs of life, in the form of flattened plants and snapped branches. They didn't have to wait long before they found something.

"Captain, sir." Moose called, after they had stopped and decided to move in an extended line, to cover more ground. "I've got something here."

Jones and Peter turned towards Moose, who bent down and picked up a blood covered M-16 rifle. Moose looked at the gun and his eyes widened. He stared at the others, his body frozen it would seem.

"Move out. Stevens can't be far. We need to find him and send him back so he can get treatment." Captain Jones ordered, clutching his gun in a white-knuckled fashion.

"I've got blood here." Peter called out, not three steps later. "A lot of blood, and …" Peter's words fell still. "Captain, you need to come see this." A shudder rolled through Peter as he spoke, and he was sure the sentiment was echoed in his speech.

The three men came together and stared at what Peter had found. A severed hand lay at the base of a large plant. The blood was fresh, the wound rough. It looked as if it had been torn away rather than removed with any form of implement.

"What the hell did this?" Moose asked

Something rustled in the trees behind them. Spinning around, his rifle at the ready, Moose gave a groan. Whatever it was, was gone again. Peter stood up straight and listened. Whatever it was circled them, the same way he had been circled earlier.

"It doesn't matter what did it, we need to find Stevens, and find a place for the second group to land. We have seven minutes, and counting. Let's go." Jones said, turning his back on the severed arm.

The jungle gave no indication as to where Stevens could have gone. There was no disturbed ground to warn them of a struggle or direction for flight.

"Stick together, they can't be far." Jones moved off, and the others followed. They stuck in a close formation, no more than a meter apart, shoulder to shoulder. As they walked, the rustling followed them. They stopped, and the rustling stopped.

"Whoever is out there, show yourself." Moose ordered. The games were wearing on his nerves. His agitation was to be heard in his short, sharp breaths.

It seemed to work, because whatever was following them stopped. A strange rasping sound came in response. It sounded like a choked purr; like a lion preparing to roar.

"Moose, come on, we need to find Stevens." Jones reach out and put a hand on the soldiers shoulder, but Moose didn't move.

"I can see it" He mumbled through clenched teeth.

"See what…" Peter asked, but Moose silenced him.

"Look." He mumbled, and both Peter and Captain Jones looked through the trees. It took them a second, but they saw it. Something was watching them. Its orange eye stared through the foliage at the same height as their own.

"What the heck…" Jones spoke in disbelief. The eye was clearly not human, not even remotely. Behind them, something shifted, something else. "We're surrounded." Jones' words were cold and emotionless. He was stating a fact, and they all knew what it meant.

At that moment, the GPS in Jones's pocket gave a series of beeps. The time was counting down, and the five minute warning had sounded. They needed to fix a location soon. It was the window they needed because the noise seemed to startle whatever it was that was watching them.

"Shoot whatever you see," Jones ordered as he spun around. The creature leaped from the trees towards him, and he opened up a burst of his M-16. Bullets tore into the scaly flesh, and the scent of fresh blood filled the air.

"What the…" Peter began, but an identical creature leaped at him. He too fired a wild burst at the leaping reptile. A second spray found their target, tearing into the creature's throat. It fell to the floor, landing on its side. Peter stumbled backwards, his brain unable to piece together what it was being shown.

Moose screamed. He too had been attacked, but he had not been fast enough to fire his weapon. He gave a cry and turned to run. His hands were pressed against his belly, but it was not enough to hold in his organs. The gash ran from side to side slicing through his military attire.

"Moose!" Peter called, but the creature rose behind his friend, its orange eyes staring at Peter. It opened its mouth and in a quick movement, bit down on Moose's head, removing it with minimal effort. The sharp teeth and the giant mouth made quick work of the morsel they had claimed, crunching down on flesh, bone and brain.

Captain Jones had witnessed the assault and had the wherewithal to grab Peter by the scruff of his neck. "Run." He ordered, shoving Peter in the direction he wanted to go. Behind them, the two creatures gave a barked cry and took after them.

A few meters into the jungle, Peter and Jones found the first half of Stevens. His lower body lay in a pool of blood and spilled organs. A long tail of intestines snaked through the grass as if trying to escape the scene. They jumped over the lower body of their fallen colleague and ran as hard as they could. The creatures were all around them. Not in pursuit, but on the hunt. They overtook the pair, the bushes shuddering as they passed. Their growls further evidence of their anger.

"That way," Captain Jones shouted, pointing to the left. "They are ahead of us now." He offered no further explanation, but veered through the tree cutting across the path their hunters had taken.

It didn't take long for them to find what remained of Stevens. His face had been split down the middle, the bone cleaved through so that globs of brain matter had seeped through the gash. His face was unrecognizable, especially at the speed with which they passed him, but it was clear enough from the uniform who the corpse was.

Their change of direction gave them a few precious seconds advantage, but they soon heard the angry cry of their pursuers, and soon the jungle was alive behind them with the sound of their advance.

The GPS device gave another series of beeps. "Three minutes." Jones called, as if explaining the sound was some form of saving grace. That in three minutes this would all be over.

The jungle stopped suddenly, and the two soldiers found themselves stuck on the edge of a cliff. The vertical drop led into a large pool of water. It looked impossibly blue from their height, and the collection of jagged rocks that lay beneath their feet was a less than comforting thought.

"They're here." Jones whispered. He and Peter stood side by side, their backs to the cliff. Both could see the creatures that were chasing them. The vegetation was not as thick near the ledge. It didn't matter anymore anyway. The game was over. The prey had been cornered, and now it was time to play.

"Jump," Peter whispered, as a cold wave of foreboding washed through is body.

"What?"

"Jump, it's the only way. Now!" He ordered to his captain. Rank held no meaning anymore.

Peter didn't wait, and neither did Jones. They leaped together in uncoordinated synchronicity. The moment they leaped, the creatures sprang from the bushes. Only rather than finding their prey, they collided with one another, and exchanged a series of angry barks.

Peter fell and closed his eyes. If he was going to land on the rocks, he did not want to see it coming. He braced himself for the impact with the water, but when it came, he was not ready.

His body crumpled from the force of the impact. A whirring jolt of numbness shot through him. He gasped, and ice cold water filled his lungs in a second. The water was deep and seemed to suck Peter down beneath the surface, no matter how hard he tried to fight it.

Dropping his rifle, and struggling out of his backpack, he kicked as hard as he could, fighting against the cold and burning in his lungs.

He felt dizzy and tired, but just as he was about to stop struggling he broke the surface. Gasping for air, coughing and spluttering, he treaded water and tried to regain his composure. Looking up he saw the two creatures staring down at him, and for a moment he thought they were going to jump down and continue their chase.

Jones had surfaced a few meters away and was staring at the same spectacle. Peter looked at him, and their eyes met. "Those are fucking dinosaurs." Peter was unable to keep his voice calm. Even though they both knew it was the truth, there was something about hearing the words said aloud that made him feel crazy.

"What is this place?" Jones asked, looking around.

"Captain, we need to get out of the water." Peter interrupted him. "We need to get out now!" He shouted, and began to frantically pull himself to the shore.

Jones looked over at Peter and saw the large shape that was floating in the water between them. A long, scaled snout as long as a man rose from the water. Another portion of the head emerged above the surface, and yellow eyes the size of footballs stared at him. The creature gave a snort and nostrils the size of grapefruit flared.

Jones swam, he forced everything from his mind and swam. The GPS was beeping in his pocket. Somehow it had survived the fall, and the water. The others would be arriving any second. He didn't need the extra impetus to get to the shore, but knowing reinforcements were on the way gave him a strange sense of calm, which added a power and purpose to his strokes. Heaving himself out of the water and onto the shore he grabbed the GPS device and slammed it into the ground. It stopped beeping and unfolded itself into a large square of circuit boards and electronics.

A wind rushed across the shore, and for a second, Jones could hear the other side, the real world, where he knew the warden would be standing waiting. He wanted to shout. To scream and ask if they had any idea what was out there, but he couldn't. The creature, which resembled a crocodile only it was as large as a bus and as wide as one too, sprang from the water. Its colossal weight crashed down onto the dirt shore. The ground shook from the impact. Giving a roar, the creature advanced, quick for its size.

At the same time, the others arrived. Phillip Wilson, a man who Jones had known for many years, was the unlucky one to arrive in the path of the creature. He never saw his death coming, for the jaws, which had been angrily snapping at the air, were already closing around him before he had truly arrived. He gave a cry, more of surprise than pain, and then he was gone.

Moving on instinct, Jones sprang to his feet, and grabbed Stuart Peart. Ripping open his bag, he grabbed the grenade he knew was in there, pulled the pin and turned to face the beast. Its jaws were drooling crimson as it made several rough chomps on Wilson's body. Timing his throw, Jones hurled the grenade into the creature's mouth and hit the deck.

"Get down," he roared as he fell to the floor. He landed with his hands over his head, and felt the others land beside him.

The blast was an almighty crack, even from within the creature's closed jaws. Jones felt the warm globs of sizzling flesh shower around them, but paid it no mind. Rolling onto his back he looked at the creature. It was dead. What had once been its head was burst open, the skull shattered, flesh and bone fragments blown backwards over the body like the skin of a peeled banana.

"What the hell, Captain." Peart cried out, picking himself out of the mess of dinosaur brain.

"Sorry man, there wasn't a lot of time to explain." Jones answered as he got to his feet. He brushed himself clean and then looked at the men who stood around him. "There is something about this place that they didn't tell us," he began.

"What, like there are giant crocodiles waiting to eat us." Peart replied his voice filled with an angry sarcasm.

"Not just crocs, but something else." Peter began, but being the youngest in the group he was shot down with a dirty look.

"The rookie is right. There are… this place is filled with dinosaurs." Jones looked his men in the eye as he spoke, in the hope that it would convey the seriousness of what he had said. "Stevens and Moose are gone. They got taken out up there, on the top of the cliff. The dinosaurs…"

"Raptors." Peter interrupted. "They were raptors." He ignored the looks that were shot his way.

"The raptors, chased us to the cliff. We jumped just before you guys arrived. We are running blind here, so I suggest we make a camp, check our equipment and take stock of things. This isn't just a retrieval anymore. I lost my communicator in the water, and Wilson had the second. We are stuck here for the seventy-two hours.

"What do you mean stuck here?" Peart gasped.

"Exactly that. The secondary protocol is that after three days we are extracted. I have a device implanted into my wrist that will track us. Providing we are all together three days from now, we will all be brought back home." Jones explained. He had a tense look on his face, and Peter understood why the warden had wanted him to watch the man.

"Wait a second, Captain. You're telling us that we are trapped in a world of dinosaurs. What about the prisoners?" Lawrence James asked.

"I don't know, I think they are here. It would explain why so many would die. We assumed it was a gang deal, but now I'm not so sure." Jones answered. He had been so busy trying to stay alive he had not even thought about the prisoners.

"So we just sit here and wait for three days," Michaels spoke up. "I mean, without the communicators we can't hope to find the guy we are after, and I highly doubt he will be waiting for us with open arms, even if he is up for release.

A mumble went around the men, who were still recovering from the abrupt change of pace they had witnessed since their arrival.

"We make camp here, find our bearings and then we head out. We will be a sitting duck out here." Jones answered. "We are going to look for this man and we will bring him home. Our orders have not changed. The mission stands." The captain ordered as he fished a fresh rifle out of the supply box. He reached in and pulled out a second rifle and offered it to Peter. "Thanks." He whispered as he handed him the weapon. He didn't need to say any more. Peter understood perfectly.

"Captain!" Micahels shouted.

They all turned to look at the man, but their eyes were taken by the giant winged creature that was swooping down towards them. Its bald body and long wings screeched as it swooped through the air. A long thin beak opened and without landing it tore away a deep strip of flesh from the dead beast.

It soared into the sky and was replaced by another, and above that circled yet more. Peter counted seven in total, each one waiting their turn for the feast.

"Move for the trees." Jones called. "Peart, Michaels, grab what you can and move out." He pointed at the two men who were closest to their supply chest. "The rest of you, fall back. Rookie, you and James lay down covering fire. I don't want to lose anybody else today. I'll clear the trees." Jones broke into a run, sprinting into the trees.

Grabbing his gun, Peter waited and as a smaller creature swooped in, its head turned towards the live prey, he opened fire. Bullets tore holes into the thing's skin covered wings and it gave a pained cry before crashing into the water.

James also released a burst but his shots bounced off the torso of a larger creature, and only served to anger it.

"Fall back." Peter called out as three more creatures descended on them. Peter raised his weapon and fired another burst into the sky, but it was no good.

James was beside him in no time. Peart and Michaels followed him. They ran past the two, who backed up towards the trees as fast as they could go, firing staggered bursts into the creatures. They made it to the trees, and turned to sprint after the others. They found them deeper in the vegetation, shaken; sweat gleaming on their exposed flesh.

"What's going on?" Peart whispered. His whole body was shaking and his skin had turned white.

"Peart, Peart." Jones called, grabbing him by the shoulders. "Hold it together. We need each other out here." He ordered, and the words seemed to work.

"Sorry captain. I don't know what came over me," he apologized.

"I need you sharp out here man." Jones patted him on the shoulder. "We need to keep moving. We need to find something that will help us get our bearings. Higher ground would be good, but for now, let's just move and find a place to regroup." Jones looked at them. "We need to stabilize and come up with a plan. I'll take the lead. Peart, you and James behind me, Rookie, you and Michaels take the rear. Watch our flanks and shoot anything that moves. We are a team, and we are prepared for anything that this place throws at us." There was fire in Jones's words; they were infectious.

They moved through the jungle in silence, sticking close together, but leaving enough room to manoeuvre should it come to it. They saw no more dinosaurs, but the bugs were the size of small birds and proved to be enough of a nuisance. Stevens swatted one to the floor and stood on it, needing to put his full bodyweight behind the movement before the creature's body finally burst.

Night fell and a gloomy twilight settled over the world. The forest cooled as the sun, which was invisible behind the tall jungle canopy, sank, but the group pushed on. While they were relieved to reach nightfall without any further dinosaur incidents, they were concerned that they had also seen no sign of human life.

"I think we are in some lost world." A voice whispered in the night.

"What if they can't get us back?"

"We could be trapped here." The hushed conversation was held at a tone that everybody could hear, but in a fashion that made people comfortable enough to believe it was a secret, so they responded honestly. All but Peter and the captain. They stood together, away from the others. They had chosen to take first watch, and nobody had offered to take their place. Their trek had been long and hard, and unfortunately they had tracked back to the same pool where they had started, coming in from the other side, following the cliff that Jones and Peter had sprung from.

Everybody had been disappointed, but Jones had once again used his motivational skills to convince them all that they were in a safe zone. Possibly because whatever lived in the water had been such a threat, the dinosaurs had learned to steer clear of the area. Whatever the real reason was, they had accepted the positive side of the argument and settled down to rest.

All of the men that worked in the Kruger Correctional Probation Department were military men, and most had seen their fair share of military action. Peter and Peart had been through boot camp training but transferred straight to the corrections unit.

"They are wrong, you know." Jones spoke to Peter, his voice hushed to a real whisper.

"Who are?" Peter asked, knowing how the game was played.

"The men. They are wrong, in part at least. I don't think there is any arguing that this is a lost world. But I am sure we are in the right place. Stronger than that, I think that son-of-a-bitch warden knew all about it. That's why he is so calm about the lack of parolees from the hard timers' wing."

"How can you be so sure?" Peter asked, looking around him, to make sure that none of the others had come down to meet them.

"Because we are being watched. We have been since just before we set up camp." Jones's words were chilling.

"Why didn't you say? What if it was..." Peter began, his voice louder than either man wanted.

"Because it's not a dinosaur. I know what it is like to be followed, and to follow people. I can hear and see all the signs. We are being watched by at least five people." Jones voice lowered to the point where even Peter struggled to hear.

"Where are they?" Peter asked, looking out into the night. They had made a fire, which burned behind them, but for the rest, the only illumination was by the night sky.

"Two to the left, one the right, and I think two up in the trees. I can't tell for sure." There was concern in Jones's voice, and Peter understood why. Most of the people who got sentenced to the Hard Times wing at Kruger were some of the most violent or sadistic offenders around. They had the advantage in terms of numbers, and their knowledge of the area. They had survived with the dinosaurs and overcome, which meant they had only grown more dangerous.

"What do we do?" Peter asked, a shiver running down his spine.

"We wait, and when they come, we will fight. We have the better weapons, and we know that they are out there. That gives us the upper hand." Jones tried a smile, but both men knew it was a pointless gesture and so he abandoned it.

They sat in silence and listened to the night. The forest was alive with the sounds of the creatures they had hoped to avoid. The noise was distant, they deduced that they were in a hollow in the ground, rather than being at the foot of a cliff. The noises of the lost world collided above their head and reached them like thunder; in rolling waves of noise that confirmed a power beyond that of their own conception and understanding.

Not long before the shift changed, as his eyes were growing heavy, Peter was pulled from sleep by a sudden scurrying to his left. His mind snapped to the thought of the prisoners attacking them, and he yanked his rifle up to fire against whoever it was that advanced on them.

The sound of the commotion grew, and a scream rang out through the night. This was followed by the sound of a number of heavy thuds, a muffled shout and then the unmistakable sound of retreat. The forest came alive with the sound of bodies crashing through the trees, fleeing in a blind panic.

"Keep your wits about you." Jones offered, as he moved beside Peter. He too had his rifle held high, finger already pressing against the trigger.

Peter heard the commotion behind them, and knew the others had been ripped from their rest, but he did not look around in search of aid.

Something moved in the dark. It was small, and fast. It came at them like a beast possessed. "I need a light." Peter called, but the thing was past him, and it was not alone. More of the creatures ran through the long grass towards them. One leaped at Peter, who moved just in time. The creature landed on the ground and spun around to face him. It was no larger than a common dog, its body covered in a short fur. It stood on two hind legs, its front legs used for attack. They lashed out, slicing at the air. Gunfire rang out from behind him, as the others found their weapons and met the creatures with full force

The creature nearest to Peter lunged again, and once more Peter sidestepped its attack. There was no chance for a third attempt as a bullet shattered the creature's skull and left it a bloodied, headless mess on the floor. Captain Jones stood with his handgun before him, arm extended straight out. He looked at Peter and nodded before turning to the others.

The gunfire had died down, the camp was littered with the bodies of the strange creatures. Closer to the fire, Peter saw that their bodies were covered in brown fur and they had a short, stubby, rat like tail. Their front teeth were short and sharp, with a curve to them that made Peter think of a snake's fangs.

"Dammit to hell." James growled as they stood gathered by the fire.

"What is it James?" The captain asked.

"One of them buggers bit me is all, sir. Nothing bad, just on the hand." Jams looked at his bloodied hand in the light of the fire. His blood looked black as streaks snaked down his wrist and over his arm.

"Peart, get him cleaned up. We move at first light. We need to find this prisoner and get him out of here." Jones looked at the men, and he felt a strange sense of hopelessness run through him. Not that he would allow that to show to them, but he felt it nonetheless.

The sun rose fast, and not long after the dark began to lift, the world was lit once more. There was no dawn, no gentle start to the day. They packed their things and headed into the trees. A few feet from their camp, Jones and Peter discovered a body. He was still wearing the tattered remains of his Kruger Correctional uniform. The grey jumpsuit was ripped to shreds, a result of time rather than the fatal attack of the previous evening.

"Hold up, that's one of ours." Peart coughed as he saw the body. "You mean to tell me we've been sending criminals to the lost world all these years?"

"I think so, but forget about it. We need to stay alive. There are bigger threats out there, and these beasts are after anything they can catch. We will stick together, go back up the cliffs. I don't know where this guy is, but his reading came from the north, so I suggest we move that way and see what we find. Sitting around here is only going to get us killed." Jones spoke to the group, without moving his eyes away from the body. The face was bloated, the features swollen to a point beyond recognition. There were not clearly identifiable wounds, no deep lacerations or anything that indicated the cause of death, and it troubled him. A gnawing sensation ate away at him on the inside, but he couldn't put his finger on what it was.

The sun rose high and the heat of the forest soon caught up with them. The group headed back to the water, in the direction Jones and Peter had come from. They had seen a trail there that indicated the direction of the fleeing men from the night before. It was as good a lead as anything.

The carcass of the prehistoric crocodile had been picked at through the night. The stench that came from its rotting frame was unbearable. As they walked by, a deep humming sound caught their attention. They looked at the felled creature in time to see an enormous insect, which looked like a dragonfly rise up from inside the hollowed out chest.

It´s body was at least a meter long and its belly was swollen from the feast. Strads of bloodied flesh hung from its jaws as it regarded them, with eyes the size of cantaloupe melons.

"Keep moving." Jones instructed.

They followed the trail, which to their relief followed a steady incline. Nobody spoke, the mood over the group was one of nervous preoccupation. They jumped at every sound. The forest was alive all around them. The cries and barks of wildlife echoed through the tall trees. The sound of breaking branches would wrench their eyes to the heavens, expecting to see some beast hurtling towards them. Yet there was nothing. The creatures were there, but their world hid them from view, and it made everybody in the team nervous.

The rain came as a great relief, at first, but as the sky grew black and the fat drops turned into a torrential downpour, they realized that a fresh problem had been presented to them. The canopy above their heads blocked out the sun, but was unable to protect them from the rain. The mud underfoot became a problem, and their progress was slowed. The incline had lessened and before they knew it, they were walking on level ground, the lake visible beneath them at certain intervals.

The weather showed no signs of breaking, and the rumble of thunder promised that the worse was still to come. The muddy ground made their journey all the more tiring; sucking at their boots with every step.

"Captain." A voice called out. They turned to see Peart standing a way behind them, and on the floor, by his feet laid James.

The group ran back towards the man, who had managed to roll onto his side in the mud. His face was red and his eyes were starting to bulge in his sockets. He held his arms tightly against his chest, crossed over each other as if he were holding onto some ancient relic that he dared not let go.

"What's wrong?" Peter asked as the captain crouched down beside the unresponsive James.

"I don't know. He's still got a pulse, but..." Jones was interrupted as James fell into a fit by their feet. His body shook and his eyes rolled back into their sockets. A thick yellowish foam spewed from his mouth.

"Hold him still." Jones ordered as he and Peter fell to their knees in an attempt to restrain him.

At that moment, a loud burst of thunder exploded over their head and a streak of lightning whipped to the ground not far from where they were. This brought the jungle to life. The ground began to shake. The trees and bushes cracked and rustled as a series of howls rang out around them. The trees parted and a stampede of dinosaurs tore through them. They ranged in size from that of chickens through to horses. They ran at the men, who dove out of their way. Behind them came the reason for their flight. A large dinosaur, at least three meters to the shoulder came careening through the trees the vegetation being torn away to leave a hole tracing the creatures progress. It gave a roar, standing up straight.

Peter buried his face in the mud, trying to bury himself as deep as possible. He held his breath and waited. The dinosaur had stopped beside them. He could hear its rasped breaths, and the flare of its nostrils as it inhaled their aroma.

Peter cried into the mud as he felt the ground squelch around him. The dinosaur's hot breath snorted down on him, and in that moment he knew that he was done for. They all were. The creature nudged him in the side with its head. The blow was powerful and it took all of Peter's control not to cry out.

The dinosaur stood up and gave a roar. The sound was deafening, and for a moment it felt as if it would never stop. The creature took off at a run, the ground rumbling in its wake.

"That was close." Peart sang as they got back to their feet. Each man was covered head to toe in mud. All apart from James, whose broken and bloodied body lay in a muddy depression in the ground.

"Oh God." Peter gasped, cupping his face in his hands.

"He never stood a chance." Michaels snarled, looking down at the body. It was close to unrecognizable, the skull had been flattened, the chest crushed by the weight of the dinosaur's foot.

There was no time to reflect on the passing of another colleague, for there was movement around them again. The foliage rustled and a snake came into view. Its round head was the size of a truck wheel, and its thick body continued to emerge even after the others had turned to flee. Chancing a look over his shoulder, Peter saw the coiled creature swallowing what remained of James, its jaws stretching wide enough to swallow the man whole.

There was a moment when the jungle and the monsoon-like rain became too much for the group and they became separated. Peter saw the captain ahead of him, but a second later he was gone, swallowed by the jungle. Peter ran, following the path he believed to be true, but found nobody.

Alone, and soaked through to the skin, it did not take long for panic to set in. He looked from side to side and as the storm cracked above his head, the lightning illuminated the hulking frame of a stegosaurus but a few meters to Peter's left. The creature, uninterested in the weather and the human ogling it, was plodding through the mud. The shock of seeing the creature was enough to make Peter stumble, and he narrowly avoided a collision with a tree.

A few strides later and Peter caught a glimpse of someone in the trees. It was a fleeting glance, but unmistakably human. Running faster, his feet slapping in the mud, his balance precarious from the slick ground, Peter charged towards the others. He was moving too fast to notice the sudden slope to the ground, and as the world fell away from him, Peter slipped and fell. He careened over the ground, running, stumbling, and finally rolling head first through the trees and plants.

He came to a stop in a large muddy puddle, his rifle on the ground a few meters away from him. What separated them was a pair of worn boots. Looking up into the rain, it took Peter a few seconds to realize that the hulking mass of a man that stood before him was not wearing the green uniform of a Kruger Correctional employee but rather the grey uniform of an inmate.

"Well, look what we have here." The man snarled, looking down at Peter with a smile that screamed malicious intent.

Peter floundered in the mud, trying to find his feet, but no sooner did he get to his knees that a kick was delivered to his ribs and he was sent sprawling once more.

"Not so fast, soldier boy." Another inmate growled. A pair of hands grabbed Peter by the shoulders and he was hauled to his feet. Mud covered his face, and before it could fall from him, the first blow was delivered.

It felt as if he had been shot, the ball of white hot pain burned in his stomach and radiated outwards, leaving a dull, nauseating throb behind. Wheezing from the blow, Peter braced himself for the second, but it never came. He was still being held, his arms pinned behind his back. Peter tried to wrench his arms free, but whoever it was that held him, was strong.

"You need to let me go. You are inmate at Kruger Correctional…" Peter began but a fist silenced him. He felt his lips burst from the force of the blow, and his nose burned. He tasted blood and struggled for breath. His nose was broken, that much he knew.

"We don't got to let you go anywhere. I don't know how dumb you are, boy, but you ain't in Kansas no more." The man holding him snarled, and the group, he heard at least three different voices, began to laugh.

"I'm not alone." Peter blurted out.

"Oh, we know. We've been watching you all." The man before him spoke.

Peter's vision cleared as the initial blast of pain began to subside. The man before him was bald with an angry red scar running across his forehead. His eyes were cold, and his mouth twisted into a sneer.

"It's not every day we get to spend time with one of the guards." A weasel-like voice spoke. Peter turned his head and saw the thin, wiry man who had spoken. His long hair was slick on his scalp, but Peter could tell that it was slick with grease rather than because of the rain.

"Ain't that the truth, Gash." The large man smiled. He was missing almost all of his teeth.

"Please…please don't do…" Peter began, but at that same moment lightning struck, and with a loud crack the tree behind the group split. The trunk cracked through the middle, the wood splitting open as it traced its way towards the ground. The two halves of the tree came apart, and the section that was felled came toppling in their direction.

It gave Peter the chance he needed to escape. Timing his jump correctly, he leaped out of the way of the tree, and in doing so managed to wrench himself free from the third prisoner's grip. Peter lowered his head and ran. Only the weasel man stood in his way and a stiff shoulder tackle was enough to remove him, his feet giving way on the muddy ground. Three more strides and Peter was free.

He could hear them give chase, but also hear the now familiar sound of dinosaur contact. He glanced over his shoulder as a creature that looked like a rhinoceros came charging through the trees. The weasel man was pushed to one side and trampled in the rush, while the scar headed inmate was skewered on the dinosaur's single long horn.

Shaking its head, as if enraged at being stuck on a creature as dirty as a human, the dinosaur thrashed until the man fell free. Still alive, he screamed as blood spurted from his punctured chest. Peter didn't wait to watch for the outcome. He turned and ran, not wanting to think about the other creatures that were hiding in the trees.

The rain was beginning to let up, and the jungle was pulling back, meaning it felt less claustrophobic. Peter was still alone. He had not seen any sign of life, other than a few enormous spiders that seemed to be involved in a highly energetic mating ritual.

Peter had lost his rifle; he had never recollected it from where it had landed, but he found his movements much more fluid without the clunky thing.

The jungle stopped suddenly, and Peter found himself on a beach. Not the white sand beaches of the Caribbean, but rather a rocky stretch of land that separated jungle and sea. Jagged rocks and boulders littered the ground; a new hazard waiting at the end of each taken step.

The sea was rough as the storm continued to rage. The wind, once out of the shelter of the trees was intense, and some of the gusts were enough to make Peter slip on the slick rocks.

Above his head, large pteranodons circled, gliding on the strong winds. For a second, Peter was lost to the spectacle of it all. One of the smaller winged dinosaurs swooped down towards the sea, hurtling closer and closer to the waves, pulling up at the last second. As it rose back up to the others, another took its place, diving down towards the water, sinking even closer to the surface. Peter watched in amazement as the purposes of their game became clear. They were challenging one another, who could dive the lowest. As he watched, the fifth pteranodon sped towards the ocean, however, it never had the chance to pull back up and join the rest, for an enormous sea beast rose from the waves. The size of the creature made the diving pteranodon seem minuscule by comparison. The beast rose out of the water, its open jaws the size of a semi-truck. It snatched the prehistoric bird from the air and crashed back into the ocean once more, sending a vast wall of water in all directions.

Behind him, something skittered over the rocks. The sound of legs clacking over the ground rang out in a sudden lull in the wind. It was a lull that saved Peter's life. Turning around, Peter had just enough time to jump aside as a large stinger was launched in his direction. The creature it was attached to looked like a scorpion, only it was the size of a dog and looked as if it had been run over by a steamroller. The body was at least two feet wide and at least two meters long even with its tail curled inwards, ready to strike again. Large pincers extended from its body and snapped at Peter who again dodged the attack. Instead, the creature caught a rock, which it crushed with ease. Drawing his handgun Peter fired three shots into the creatures face. The soft flesh burst open and with a human-like scream it fell still.

Panting, Peter looked around, expecting the next creature to rear its ugly head to be the one that finally took him down. Only there was nothing. He was alone with the wind and the rain. Even the pteranodon's above him had disappeared.

The storm continued to rage, and the world became so dark, it was impossible to gauge what time of day it was.

Peter picked his way across the rocks, staying close to the jungle. He knew that in spite of the danger it was filled with, the trees offered him the most protection and at the same time, the best chance of survival.

Between the trees the wind fell away and while the rain was still falling hard, the fact that there was a canopy overhead made it feel as if the worst was over. Peter was soaked to his skin, and knew that he needed to find shelter if he wanted to survive the storm. His visibility was significantly reduced, and with nothing but a hand gun to defend himself with, Peter did not like his odds of coming out on top.

`Luck was on his side when he came across a fallen tree. It was clear that the felling had not been the result of the storm. The trunk was smashed and splintered. What interested him however, was the large bird's nest which lay on the floor ahead of him. It was at least two meters across and would provide the perfect amount of shelter.

The nest was stuck in the mud, part buried but Peter managed, with some effort, to free it and flip it over. Crawling underneath he curled up. The ground was wet and the mud seeped through his clothes, but the nest protected him from the rain, and hid him from what was out there. He didn't want to think about the squashed body of James, nor the way the charging rhino beast had trampled the prisoners he had met.

Peter hadn't realized until after he was safe, how tired he was. Exhausted would be the better word for it. He hadn't slept in close to two days, and had been on the run ever since he arrived. While his mind refused to calm, overloaded from the things it had seen since arriving, Peter's body began to shut down, and soon he fell into a troubled, and tiring sleep.

Wrenched from slumber by the sound of splintering wood, Peter work with a jolt, lost and confused, he felt like he was going to vomit. Rolling onto his side, Peter wretched until his side burned with cramp. He shivered with cold, from having lain in the muddy ground for so long. His head pounded and his body ached. The thought of moving was enough to make him groan.

The sound of something heavy impacting against the trees around him rocked the world once more. Peering out from under the nest, Peter looked around. He could see nothing, but his view was limited. Pushing the nest up, Peter slowly crawled out. The rain had stopped and a low level mist hung around the trees. The humidity had soared as a result and Peter was sweating before he had so much as gotten to his feet.

Behind him, something grunted, and the ground shook once more. Turning, he stumbled backwards, a yell stuck in his throat. Two triceratops were standing not fifteen feet away from him. They were rutting with one another. The impact of their collisions was what shook the ground and the close proximity of the trees and their close quarters combat had resulted in several trees being badly damaged. The trunk of one had been split in half; the tree only remaining upright thanks to the support of its neighbours.

"Psst" A voice called out. "Pssst. Over here." Peter looked around, but saw nothing. "Up here." The voice called again. This time Peter rose his gaze and soon saw who was calling him. A face stared at him from up in the trees.

"Who.." Peter asked, but the man silenced him with an agitated cut-throat gesture.

"Move slowly. Don't make a sound. They are horny and will kill anything that gets between them and the female." The man spoke and his head disappeared.

For a moment Peter wondered if he had imagined it all, but when the man appeared again, at ground level, Peter had no real option but to trust him.

Peter moved slowly. The ground, while already beginning to harden, still made silent movement an awkward thing to attempt. Peter looked over his shoulder and waited. He saw the two triceratops preparing to charge one another again, and the moment they made their move, so did he. Darting into the trees, Peter was swallowed by a patch of large fern bushes which towered above his head.

At first there was no sign of the man who had called to him. Peter turned a full circle, and then he appeared. He was hesitant. His eyes were darting around, moving from place to place, only it was not the ever cautious gaze of a man ready to fight at any moment, but rather the quick nervous movements of a man afraid for his life.

He was wearing the grey uniform of an inmate, what was left of it at least, but did not have the same attitude as the previous group Peter had encountered.

"You're an officer right. One of the guards?" The man whispered, his voice almost inaudible.

"Yes. We came in to find an inmate and bring him home." Peter answered, lowering his own voice after seeing the way the man flinched at the initial volume of his reply.

"You came here alone?" The man sounded shocked.

"No, we came with a whole unit. Two groups in fact. But we got attacked by the …" He paused, realizing for the first time the reality of what he was about to say.

"The dinosaurs. It's alright, it takes a little bit of getting used to." The man smiled.

"Yeah, it came as a bit of a shock. We arrived and were hunted by a group of raptors within seconds.

"You got away from the raptors? Nice moves. Must have been yours I heard throwing around the ammunition yesterday." He nodded to himself, agreeing with his statement.

"Who are you?" Peter asked, but the man carried on as if he had not heard him.

"You guys didn't know about this place?" His interest was genuine; his head cocked to one side in anticipation of the answer.

"Well, yes and no. We knew that they were sending the hard time… the inmates somewhere, especially those in the Alpha block, but we had no idea what else was here." Peter answered honestly.

"Well, we had better move. You think their fights are noisy, you should be here to see what the winner does to the female." The man winked, gave a gentle laugh and then was gone. He moved through the trees like a ghost.

Peter tried his best to follow, but continued to lose sight of the man, and twice got called back on course after having doubled back on himself.

"How can I trust you?" Peter asked as they stopped beneath the base of a large tree. There were deep gouges made into the trunk, which Peter mistakenly took for further evidence of dinosaur activity.

"You can't, but now that you're all alone, I guess you don't have a choice." The man answered. His reply was short and to the point. He was gone in a second, scaling the tree. It was then that Peter realized the grooves were not claw marks, but steps. The man had brought Peter to that place not because it was a convenient place to rest, but with a purpose. "I wouldn't stay down there for too long, chief." The man called down once he was half way up the tree.

"Why's that." Peter asked, getting a sense that there was something he was not being told. An image appeared in his mind of a group of prisoners waiting for him up in the trees. Ready to jump him and string his body from the branches.

"Because they are hungry." He answered with a laugh, and resumed his climb.

Peter turned around and saw a giant lizard emerge from the trees. It moved slowly, with thoughtful steps. It reminded Peter of a Komodo dragon, only it was the size of a large van. The creature rose its head, and a long forked tongue, the colour of coal, flicked from its mouth. It turned towards Peter and gave an angry hiss.

Not wanting to see the creature any closer than he already had, Peter leaped up the trunk, deftly navigating the crudely fashioned ladder, even if the distance between the manmade grooves was irregular and uncomfortable.

Once he reached the top he found another large nest, larger than the one he had camped beneath the night before. The prisoner who had saved him was already sitting on the mass of twigs and fern.

"It's safe. These things are built to hold babies that weigh more than you and I." The man said, stretching out as if lounging on a sofa. "It's not too bad once you get used to it. Of course, you guys are new. Me, I've been here a long time." There was a note to the man's voice that put Peter on edge. "You see, when you're out here, the rules are changed. Kill or be killed. That's what they all say." Slowly, Peter reached for his sidearm. "Don't worry about shooting me. I ain't no threat to you. I ain't killed nobody, not before I got in here, and not since." The man smiled and his face changed. He was a middle aged man, whose hair was long and his beard crudely trimmed. His eyes were a deep auburn and still held the life that had been missing from the first group of prisoners Peter had met.

"How long have you been here?" Peter asked, figuring that it was as good a lead in question as could be asked.

"It's easy to lose track of things over here. But my sentence was fifteen years." The man looked around him. "Time loses all meaning out here. I'm sure they have all said it before, but it's true."

"All who?"

"The prisoners that have served their time and gone home."

Peter fell silent. He sat in the nest, and struggled to find a position that was comfortable. "Nobody has ever made it out." He said in a whisper.

"Then why are you here now?" The man squinted as he looked at Peter, his eyes searching for the truth.

"We are here to bring out a man who has served his sentence. It is the first time someone has made it. We always assumed that his world was just a barren place, and that..." Peter caught his words, remembering that he was talking to a prisoner.

"You thought we were all just animals, hunting each other down. Survival of the fittest." He laughed. "Bet you shat bricks when you saw them beasts down there, right." He pointed to the ground, where three giant lizards were digging in the muddy forest floor.

Peter peered over the side of the nest. He had not realized how far up they had climbed. "What are they doing?" He asked.

"Getting ready to lay their eggs. They do it twice a year. One egg each, always in the same place." The man stared at the animals and then looked sternly at Peter. "They will be gone in a few hours. Then we can head back down to the ground."

"Before the owners get home, right?" Peter tried to make a joke. He felt a strange urge to trust the man who had saved him, but his body ached and his face stung from the beating he had taken.

"What... oh the nest. No, this place has been empty for years. I just meant that we should get you out of here. You must have an extraction area of something. Right?" The prisoner looked at Peter as if his assumption truly was as logical as it sounded.

"It doesn't exactly work like that. Our captain, he has a tracker device on him. If we haven't signalled in three days the tracker will send a signal and we will be collected but..."

"But what?" The man couldn't help but smile at Peter. "Forgive me, it has been a long time since I had a real conversation."

"Well, out communicators got broken, and eaten. If I am going to leave this place, I need to be standing near Captain Jones."

"Then we go find him. The noise you guys made so far will make him easy to track." That smile spread across this dark skinned face once more.

"That's not all. We need to find Troy Gardner first."

"Who is he?" The man asked, sitting upright in the nest.

"He is the inmate we have come to extract." Peter answered, jumping as one of the creatures on the ground gave a startled growl.

"I've never heard of him. Is he white, black?"

"What difference does it make?" Peter asked.

"This is prison man. Dinosaurs or not, there are rules. The main one being, you stick with your own. You see the whites, they've got the hills. Those clean skinned fellas don't want to be getting dirty down in the mud. The Latino's, they have the jungle and the blacks, well, my brothers got the volcano. Yeah, you heard me right. This island got a volcano on it. Could you get any more cliché?" The man gave a sarcastic laugh.

"What about you?"

"What about me?"

"Well, you're... you're... black." Peter froze, hating the way the word sounded coming from his mouth. "But I don't see a volcano around here."

"I'm a special case. You see, I don't belong here, but at the same time, I can't ever leave. None of us can. We've been here far too long. You get conditioned to this place, and after a while, the thought of going back to the real is more terrifying than being chased by an angry T-Rex."

"Well, this Troy is black. So I guess I need to head towards the volcano." Peter mused, watching as the man reacted nervously every time he said the name.

"What you need to do is find your friends and leave. You don't want to be going down there. They will eat you alive, kid. No, you need to forget about this Troy guy, find your friends and pray to whoever it is you pray to, that you don't get eaten before its time to go home. There ain't nobody playing games out here." The man was getting more agitated in his speech; excited rather than aggressive, but it was enough to put Peter on edge.

"I can't to do that." Peter stood his ground. He had never considered himself a devoutly moral person before. The opportunity to ponder such a character trait had never truly arisen. Now, when faced with it, he understood it fully. "Troy Gardner is a man who has served his time. He has every bit the right to leave this place as I do." Peter stood up and while the nest felt uneasy to him, it held firm.

"I admire your guts kid, I really do. But this Troy, even if he is alive, he will be too institutionalized now to survive out there. You think prisoners get conditioned, you try living here.

"Well he is alive, I know it, and he deserves a chance." Peter felt a surge of emotion charge through him. Not anger, but a rousing sense of duty.

"How can you be so sure out there?"

"Every inmate has their vital signs measured. You all have a microchip in you that sends us your vitals every second of the day."

"Is that so?" The man sounded impressed.

"Yes, and Troy is the first one who has survived out here long enough to see the outside world again." Peter had no plans to sit, but a rustling in the branches behind him caused him to jump and fall.

"Those ones are fine. Friendly things." The man spoke as the large caterpillar-like creature came into view. Its body was about a foot long and several inches around. It was a strange green colour and had long antennae extending from the top of its head.

"When those creatures is done, I'll take you down, but I beg you, leave Troy alone." There was a pleading tone to the man's voice.

"I just can't do that." Peter politely refused and made himself comfortable again in the nest. His head was throbbing, and while the ache in his body had subsided, he could feel it lurking there, like a crocodile, just beneath the surface, waiting to strike at the right moment.

It took several hours before the creatures had dug their nests and each deposited a single egg, by which time the sun was beginning to set and the jungle world was getting dark.

"We'd better stay here the night. We will move once the sun is up and try to find your friends." The prisoner was lying on the base of the nest, with his back to Peter. "Try to get some rest. You don't look too good, and tomorrow is going to be an interesting day."

"Why's that?" Peter asked.

"Well, last thing I heard, before finding you, was some gunfire coming from the west. We don't have any guns around here, so I figure it was your boys. They were heading towards the plains. It's a big trek out there, and that's where they live."

"Who, inmates?" Peter saw an image in his mind of Captain Jones, Michaels and Peart all strung up from a tree branch. Prisoners standing beneath their bloodied corpses, dancing as their blood fell like a crimson rain.

"No, the rex's." The world seemed to fall silent at the mention of the king of the beasts. "That's right. Even in this world, the king gets given their space. There are a few of them, living out here on the border of the trees. They hunt on the plains. I bet you ain't seen nothing like these plains before. It's like something out of a movie, or a painting. Yes, sir. If your friends made it that far, then tomorrow will be an interesting day." The prisoners words trailed off and he fell asleep almost instantly.

Peter lay on the floor of the nest, listening to the world around him. The creaks and groans of the jungle. Every rush of air, each rattle of the leaves around him, and the distant crash of trees, ripped slumber further and further from his reach.

Exhaustion won out in the end however, and after a time, Peter fell into a deep sleep.

CHAPTER 3 – THE WAY HOME

When Peter woke the next morning, it felt as if his body were on fire. Sweat, slick and cold, swathed his body and had soaked his uniform. In spite of the heat that raged inside him, he could not stop shivering. His teeth gnashed and his whole body seemed to tremble with a force that he had no power to control.

Sitting up in the nest, Peter's head exploded. The pain made him groan, that was when he heard his inmate friend.

"You look terrible." The words were short and sharp, but the compassion conveyed in them was more than clear.

"Well, I feel it too, so I guess that's one good thing." Peter choked out a laugh. "I'll be fine. I just need to keep moving that's all.

"Sure thing boss. But we had better wait a few minutes first, unless you want to be the pallet cleanser." It was the inmates turn to laugh now.

"What do you mean?" Peter asked, and the man pointed over the side of the nest, deeming that words were not wholly appropriate to supplement what had already been said.

Crawling through the nest, Peter peered over the edge and gasped. The holes that had been dug the day before had been re-dug overnight. A large dinosaur with a squat rounded frame and what looked like a jagged turtle shell covering its enormous body, was busy munching on the second of the three eggs it had exposed. The broken remains of the first shell were clear to see in the now empty hole. The creature gave a grunt as it noticed the second egg was also finished. It moved slowly with heavy thudding steps, towards the third and final egg. Its short club-ended tail swung from side to side as it moved.

"Don't worry. That thing won't even both about us. We could be standing next to it, and it would be too stupid to notice us. It's the little buggers that follow it around that you need to watch out for. Vicious little things. Not too bad on their own, but in a group they like to play tough, and well, I've seen a few guys eaten alive by them."

Peter sat back and listened as the dinosaur crunched through the third and final egg. He felt sad for the lizards that had laid them. He wondered if they knew, or if they even came back once the eggs hatched.

"Watch this." The prisoner called, and beckoned Peter over to him. Peter moved slowly, his muscle ache had lessened but the fever that was slowly burning away inside of him was impossible to ignore.

Peter peered over the nest and watched as the large dinosaur disappeared through the trees, its tail beating the trunks as it swayed its giant frame from side to side. A few moments later they arrived. Five of the strangest creatures Peter had ever seen. They were grey in colour and the size of a Labrador. But they were thin and gangly. Long legs attached to a tiny body, upon which was perched a long neck and a strange, narrow head. The creatures were fast, and moved around the broken chunks of egg shell and scoffed at the remains they could find.

A fight broke out over the final piece, which resulted in one of the creatures being torn apart by the obvious alpha of their group.

Only once they had left did Peter and his new friend decide to attempt the climb down to the ground. It was an act much easier said than done given Peter's condition, which was deteriorating rapidly.

The world was starting to spin around him, and the sweat which had slicked his skin upon waking was back, and seemed to ooze from his every pore in a relentless tide of fluid. Leaning against the tree trunk for support, Peter waited for the ground to steady beneath his feet.

A hand clapped him on the shoulder. "You alright to do this?" The inmate asked, the concern in his voice genuine, but born through practicality. A sick man would put him at greater risk.

"Yeah, just give me a second." Peter managed to force the words out before a thick, sour smelling vomit spewed from his mouth, splattering against the bark of the tree.

"Ok, you've marked your territory, but now we should get moving. It's going to be a long day for you buddy."

They walked in silence, stopping only twice for Peter to vomit. The final time of which nothing really came out besides a frothy bile. Sweat dripped from his body, made only worse by the humidity of the forest. Twice he stumbled and fell to the ground.

"I need to rest." Peter croaked with slurred words.

"Not here we don't. You think the raptors you've escaped from were bad. You ain't seen nothing yet." The inmate gave a nervous smile and then looked around. "We're in their zone, which is not a place you want to be for long, or will be. Now get moving, because I will not be dino chow just because I took pity on a guard who had lost his way." Peter understood that the sudden change in tone was a motivational device, but damned if it wasn't effective nonetheless.

The jungle began to thin, or rather, it became less densely populated. Trees were replaced by shattered stumps. Peter walked with his head down, mostly so that he could focus on his feet, which felt as if they were not truly under the command of his mind, and so could betray him at any moment.

The first time he saw it, the small glint in a stray beam of sunlight that made it through a gap in the canopy overhead, he attributed it to the fever. His mind playing tricks on him. Soon there were more however, and before they reached the clearing, Peter already knew what he would find.

The clearing was there, as he had expected. The fear seemed to have cleared his fever a little bit, or at least forced his mind to focus fully on the task at hand; surviving in the lost world for another day, and getting home.

The signs of the fire fight became more obvious, as too did the blood, which clearly moved in two different directions.

Peter was so focused on what he was convinced lay ahead, that he didn't see what was actually there, and so walked into the back of the inmate who was helping him. Spinning round the inmate had a look of anger flash in his eyes. It cleared in a moment, but it was enough to remind Peter that whoever this man was, he was a criminal serving hard time, so whatever he did, it had been bad enough to warrant a sentence here.

"Sorry." Peter offered, and the man cringed, rushing a finger to his lips, his eyes went wide with fear, and his body tensed. He froze in place, as if scared to so much as move.

The growl that soon followed was the reason why. Looking up, and over the man's shoulder he saw a large dinosaur, one of the largest he had seen yet. It looked like the raptors that had been their welcoming committee, only much larger. Its head raised, alerted to the sound of their presence no doubt. From its giant jaws Peter could make out Michaels's body. Even when blood soaked, his bright blonde hair was unmistakable.

Peter felt a rush of anger surge through him. His fever riddled brain was replaced with a more primitive model, and the urge to charge and fight was overwhelming. That changed the minute he saw that Michaels was somehow still alive. His eyes opened, and whether he saw Peter or not, was impossible to tell, but a smile spread across his pale face. He raised his arm. In it was clutched a grenade; there had been a few in the supply box that had arrived with them.

With his final moments, Michaels pushed the grenade into the giant raptor's mouth. It was almost too quick to believe. The explosion was a muted thud, beginning within the skull of the dinosaur, but the result was effective in any case. The jaws crunched down in reflex, and the severed remains of Michaels fell to the floor. This was followed by the majority of the raptors head, which exploded in a shower of scorching flesh and shattered bone.

The creature's lower jaw disintegrated during the blast, while the rest of his head was peeled backwards like a piece of ripe fruit bursting in the heat. Flesh and bone were exposed to the air, and while the creature remained on its feet, the result was inevitable. Blood poured from the wound and fell from the mass of meat like a rain. With an almighty crash the creature forward, and after a few paces in an attempt to keep its balance, it fell to the floor.

"I've never seen that before." The inmate with Peter commented, impressed at what he had seen. "You got any of those?" He asked, hopeful.

"No, why?" He asked, but the answer came to him almost immediately. "There's more of them right?"

"Oh yeah, these things move in a pack." The man had no time to speak, when a growl, a much closer one, rumbled by them.

The trees shook, and out of nowhere, or so it seemed to them, a giant raptor appeared. The first thing that Peter noticed was the feet. Three long claws dug deep into the muddy ground, while a fourth rose above the others. It was a thick curled claw that looked more like a sword. It would have looked comically out of place had it not been attached to a living, breathing dinosaur.

"What do we do?" Peter asked, hoping for some absurdly simple answer, like stand still, or play dead.

"Run like the wind." The inmate whispered, and was gone.

Peter did the same, choosing a different route. It was an automatic decision based on survival and nothing more. If they went in two directions, the creature would have to choose. That plan worked, but he was the target that the raptor decided to follow.

Peter sprinted over the clearing, forcing his legs to listen to his demands. The creature burst through the trees with a roar, and came thundering after him. Peter knew he had no choice but to keep moving, and so lowered his head and willed himself to run even faster.

It was a fruitless endeavour because the dinosaur was closing ground on him with each large, powerful stride. Stumbling, his legs tied beneath him, Peter felt himself pitch forward. He tried to keep his balance but fell. As he tumbled to the floor, he saw that he had fallen over Michael's head, which had been blown from the body as a result of the grenade exploding.

Bracing himself for the inevitable, Peter tensed. But nothing came. The dinosaur gave a roar, and this was followed by a series of lesser barks and hissed shrieks. Changing a glance up from the floor, Peter looked on as a number of small dinosaurs, each one twice the size of him, attacked the larger creature. Jumping through the air they landed on its body, gouging chunks of flesh free in a frenzy of claws and teeth.

The large raptor shook its head and one of the dinosaurs was shaken loose. It fell to the floor and was promptly cut clean in half by the large claw on the raptors foot.

"Run fool. Those things will eat you too." A voice called from the trees on the other side of the clearing. Looking up, Peter saw the face of his new friend through the trees. Summoning all of the strength he had left inside him, Peter pushed himself to his feet and sprinted towards the trees. His head was exploding and his stomach churned. His desire to vomit was almost equal to his desire to survive, or so it felt in those final moments before the trees consumed him offering at least a modicum of safety, as the battle waged on.

Looking over his shoulder, back into the clearing, Peter saw that the raptor had somehow taken the upper hand and seemed to be fighting one on one with the final smaller creature.

"Well look at what we got here." A deep, drawling voice growled. Peter turned around and was met by a fist which put him on his ass in the mud.

Stunned by the attack, and blinded by the tears that came as a result of the blow, Peter was lost. As his vision cleared, the first thing he saw was his friend, the man who had saved him from being eaten, only to deliver him into the arms of a group of convicts.

"How could you…" He began, but then the rest of the scene came into focus. He saw the two men standing on either side of his friend. He saw the knife held at the man's throat. There was a distinct look of terror in the man's eyes, born not only through fear for his own life.

"Shut up fool." A voice snapped again. "You're a guard. You know the way off this goddamned island." The voice growled. Peter turned his head and saw the man.

He was an older man, his onyx skin as hard as leather. His hair was long and wild, his beard thick and overflowing. His eyes burned and even twinkled as he stared at Peter. His head was twisted to the side. He didn't blink. Not once. He merely bored a hole through Peter with his stare.

Peter looked at the man and knew that he was staring into the eyes of madness.

A smile broke on the man's face. Broken, yellow teeth appears in his beard. He licked his lips and gave a laugh.

"I don't know how to get off this island." Peter began. "It doesn't work like that." He stumbled over the words.

Behind them the giant raptor gave a triumphant roar as it defeated its final assailant. The Troodons had left their mark however, and the beast trudged back into the trees on the other side of the clearing.

"Listen Captain fucking courageous, I'm not playing games. We're getting out of here, and you are taking us." The man spoke, leaning in close to Peter. The stench that he produced did nothing to help settle Peter's queasy stomach.

"No." Peter found the word coming from his mouth before he realized it.

The refusal seemed to stagger the group, and gave Peter the chance he needed to get to his feet and draw his sidearm. He swayed on his feet and his vision was slowly spinning from fever, but the gun was enough to swing the odds in his favour, albeit momentarily.

Peter moved his gun from one target to the other. He saw six men in total, not including his ally.

"I don't think you want to be firing that around here." The bearded man continued to smile. "Besides, you fire that thing, and we'll kill you. So put it down and think with your head. We want out of this place, and you're going to bring us. It's that simple." The man spread his arms and threw his head back, and the others in the group gave a murmur of agreement.

Peter steadied his hand and moved his finger over the trigger. It was a slight movement, but got their attention. "You're not getting out of here. You are here for a reason." Peter spat. "You are criminals, hard timer's. You got your trial and you got what you deserved. If your time is ever up, then we will come and get you too."

Something twinkled in the bearded man's eyes. "Who are you here for?" He sneered.

"You expect me to tell you?" Peter replied.

"How else will you find your man?"

"What makes you think…" Peter began, but he was cut off.

"Don't play me for the fool. They wouldn't send you in, unless it was to bring someone out. They don't care about us until then. We're a dirty little secret don't you know." The bearded man leaned in even closer, and Peter saw something crawling in his beard. "Besides, it's not like I am asking you to suck my dick or anything. Not yet at least." The man laughed and around them the group of inmates laughed too. Leaning in closer still, the man licked his lips and gave Peter a wink.

In the next moment, a streak of red marred the man's face. Blood dribbled from his mouth and caught in his beard. Without saying another word the bearded man fell to his knees. That was when Peter saw him. Captain Jones emerged from the trees, his rifle at the ready. Four more shots took out the remaining prisoners. All apart from Peter's assistant. Jumping towards the man, Peter threw his arms wide. "He's with me."

Captain Jones held his fire, but refrained from taking his finger from the trigger. Peter saw then that his left arm was coated with dried blood. He looked rusty.

"We need to move, now. They are not far behind me." Jones panted.

He looked at Peter, and what Peter saw was not the commanding officer he had arrived with, but the hollow shell of a man who had seen more than he should. While Peter, in a strange morbid way had accepted that death was all around them, he was starting to see the true beauty and wonder of the world. The captain was clearly struggling with everything.

"We can't go that way. There is an angry giant raptor waiting in the trees. We pissed it off a little." Peter threw his head back towards the clearing. "What is chasing you?" He asked with a genuine interest.

"A group of about fifty angry men, who are equal parts horny and homicidal." The captain looked over his shoulder as he spoke, as if expecting another group of prisoners to come bearing down on them.

"What happened?" Peter asked. "Where is Peart?"

"They got him. They took us in the night. We tried to escape. Michaels made it, but Peart..." Tears streaked the captain's dirt encrusted face.

"They killed him?" Peter drew his own conclusions.

"Eventually, yes," Jones lowered his eyes to the floor, and Peter understood enough not to push for any more answered.

"Michaels is gone too. The raptor got him; the first one did anyway. He blew it up with a grenade." Peter felt the need to point out Michaels' heroism.

"Follow me. I can keep you safe." The prisoner spoke, pulling Jones' attention, and itchy trigger finger back into the present.

"Who is this?" Jones demanded.

"I'm just…"

"This is Troy Gardener." Peter answered. He didn't look at Jones, but at the prisoner who had saved his life, and looked set to do it again.

"How did you know?" He asked, his eyes watching Peter.

"You as good as told me." Peter answered and Troy smiled at him, nodding his head in a gentle, appreciative movement.

"Very nice, well done, good find. Let's get moving." Jones spoke, as the voices of his pursuers echoed through the trees.

"Follow me." Troy spoke, and took off. He ran through the trees, darting among the ferns and the plants, not following any clear pathway. Jones and Peter tried hard to keep up, but they continued to get caught in the foliage. Behind them, the shouts of prisoners echoed. Neither man turned their heads, for both knew what they would see coming charging through the trees.

"Psst, this way." A voice called and they looked up. High in the trees, Troy looked down at them. "Quick, get up here."

Peter knew what to look for, and no sooner had his eyes settled on the grooves in the trees trunk, he was climbing up into the thick green leaves. He heard Jones call up to him, but by the time he reached the assumed safety of the foliage, his captain was half way up the tree.

"Give me your hand." Troy spoke, reached down towards Jones.

Hesitating, Jones eventually extended a hand and was hauled into the green and out of sight. Not thirty seconds later, a group of prisoners ran through their field of view. They were armed with sticks and primitive knife-like weapons.

"Keep quiet." Troy whispered to them both.

The position in the tree was not as comfortable as the nest of the previous night, but it was better than nothing. Wrapping both arms around the trunk, Peter closed his eyes and counted backwards. The last thing he wanted was to give away their position by vomiting on the heads of the men below.

While oblivious to their presence above their heads, the criminals huddled by the base of the tree. They held their weapons ready. Something had caught their attention. A few moments later a giant creature ambled into view. It was the size of a cow and looked like an ant-eater. It was shuffling through the shrubs, its nose buried in the ground, stopping every now and then when it caught the scent of something good.

It appeared to pose no real threat to the men, but their attention was held by it. The creature stood still and raised its head. It studied the men for a second, and gave a piercing shriek. Charging the group at a speed that belied its size, the creature became a snarling dervish of teeth and claws.

The men scattered, several threw their clubs at the creature, but they did nothing to deter its attack. One man was caught in the creature's path. He was ripped to shreds, his guts spilled to the floor. The creature, seeing its target defeated, showed no interest in feeding from its kill. Instead it turned on the nearest member of the group. The man turned to run, but was easily chased down. He and the creature charged through the low leaves, but the scream that rang out a few moments later confirmed that his fate had been sealed.

A short time later, the creature appeared again. It walked over to its original position and resumed snuffling through the ground. It sniffed at the pool of blood near the still dying prisoner, who was trying in vain to push his insides back through the hole they had spilled from. It gave a grunt, as if disgusted by the aroma, and turned to walk back through the trees, snorting as it went.

"Thanks." Captain Jones looked at Troy and gave him a curt appreciation.

"Hey, you're my ticket out of here." Troy smiled. Peter heard the humour in Troy's voice, but it was lost on Jones, who clearly only saw the man as a con.

"Don't get your hopes up." Jones snapped. "I've lost a lot of good men chasing you." He growled.

"Relax man, I'm joking. This place is a horror world. You gotta be able to keep smiling at something." Troy offered an explanation, but Jones swept away his attempt at conversation.

"Well, in a few hours we will be out of here. This will be done and you will be a free man." Jones looked Troy up and down.

"Six hours can be a long time out here." Troy answered.

"Well, let's just hold tight up here. We can wait it out." Jones didn't look at Troy, or Peter, who was holding onto the branch the same way he held onto his consciousness, loosely. Jones stared at the body on the floor. The man was still alive. Shivering and gasping for air.

"You have no idea about this place do you?" Troy couldn't help but sneer. "You can't stay anywhere for a few minutes, let alone hours, even up here in the trees.

"What do you mean?" Jones asked, turning his head to look at Troy.

"Those things don't just live on the ground." That was all Troy offered. "We should get back down," he added almost as an afterthought.

"Why, I think we should hold it out as long as we can." Jones looked at Troy, and the man who had made the lost world his home saw something. He saw fear in the man's eyes.

"Well, I want to get down before he falls. I like the guy, and don't want to see him end up a pancake. Plus, I'd like to get down before we piss those guys off any more than we already have. Troy pointed through the trees to where three pairs of eyes stared at them.

Captain Jones gave a groan. His capacity for surprise had been reduced to the point where the best he could muster was a numb feeling of pessimistic acceptance. "They don't look too scary." He added. "We can take them out. Wait up here. I've got a GPS tacker in me, under my skin. In six hours we are out of here, and as long as you are with me, you will be too. So don't try scaring me, or pulling any funny business." His dislike of Troy was evident, but Troy let it slide. His anger simmered beneath the surface, but he knew that it was something he would have to get used to if he were truly going to be a free man.

"Fine, have it your way. Those things won't eat you, but we are in their territory, and that is reason enough for them to fight us off. The beasts run this world. You need to understand that. Even if it is just for six hours." Troy spat, releasing a little bit of the fire he felt. Just enough to reduce the pressure.

Jones didn't move, he watched the dinosaurs, which had inched closer to them. They were close to a meter long, and their skin was covered with feathers. Their snouts were rudimentary beaks. One gave a strange squawk, and Jones saw the row of tiny teeth that lined the inside of their bills.

One made its move. It leaped from one tree to theirs. Wings appeared between its spread arms and legs as it sailed to them. It landed on the end of the branch above them, tucking its blue feathered wings away. Sharp claws sprouted from the end of each of its four limbs and cut into the branch of the tree as it found purchase.

"I'm going first, don't want you pulling some funny business as I'm coming down." Jones growled as he pushed Troy out of the way. He paid no attention to Peter, whose sweat drenched body still clung weakly to both consciousness and the tree.

"I'm here for you buddy." Troy said, moving to Peter to help him down. "I thought all you guards were assholes like him, but you, you're different. Stay awake for me now." Troy continued talking to Peter, who offered no direct response but seemed to listen to the voice that addressed him.

Moving down the tree with a sluggish and unbalanced guard above him was no easy task, but Troy made it to the ground, as did Peter, without the help of Jones. The captain stood waiting for them. He held a small firearm at the ready, and had a wild look in his eyes. It was a look that Troy recognized. He had seen it in enough people over the years.

"You're a captain, right?" Troy asked once he was standing. He had Peter's arm over his shoulder and was bearing most of his bodyweight also.

"What business it that of yours." Jones snapped.

"Just trying to start a conversation man. If we are going to survive out there, we need to be on the same page. That's why I'm out here alone. Ain't nobody on the same page as me. They only interested in fighting back..." Troy stopped when Jones's head swivelled round to face him. Had the human neck been allowed to rotate further than it did, there was a chance that Jones you have snapped his own neck the speed with which his head spun.

"So you are some kind of pacifist?" Jones growled, trying but failing to keep his voice down. "You are not a man who was put here for killing a man in cold blood?" Jones turned so that the rest of his body also faced Troy. "I came here with men that I have worked with since our tours of duty. They died because your murdering ass has been granted parole. You make me sick. If it were up to me, I would leave you here to rot." Jones made a move as if to lunge at Troy. Troy didn't move. He stood stock still and watched Jones.

"But you haven't. Why? Because you know the truth about what happened. Because deep down you know that if some drunk wiped out your wife and kid, you would hunt them down and do exactly the same thing I did. You are stuck here, and you are scared. I'm sorry your men died, but maybe you can understand what it is like to live out here. They can't keep people like this. Prisoners or not. You know that. That is why you are still standing here. You are afraid, you are scared and you are alone. You need me more than I need you, so shut the hell up and help me with you colleague here. Otherwise, we might just leave you behind. It won't take long for this world to finish you off, and we can pick that damned tracker out from your carcass and be home for dinner." Troy knew he was shouting, he knew that it would only attract the wrong kind of attention, but he didn't care. He exploded and felt instantly better for it.

Jones stood as if he had been slapped in the face. He didn't know what to say, or what to do. "What's your plan then?" He grumbled, the respect present in his voice, but masked by a mournful cry of damaged masculinity.

"We keep moving, and hope for the best. It's the only plan that works in this place.

"Fine, then we stick to the trees, stay undercover." Jones began, and it was the last thing Troy wanted to do, but he needed to interrupt the plan.

"That would work if we were trying to hide from the other prisoners. But they are the least of our problems. You must see that. We need to stick to the path. Move out into the open. We need to get out of the trees. Not many people venture too far out there." Troy countered, offering his plan in spite of the knowledge that it was driving an even bigger wedge between him and the man that offered him his safety.

"If people don't go out there, why should we?" Jones studied Troy who was still supporting Peter, who was slowly coming too.

"Just trust me." Troy smiled at Jones, hoping that he could appeal to the man a little, but it was the wrong move.

"I don't trust you as far as I can spit. We will stick to the trees. Move back the way we came. There was water back there. We can rest and clean up." Troy opened his mouth to offer another retort, but closed it when he saw the resolved look on Jones's face.

"It's your funeral man. I'm already at home here." Troy stepped back and bowed his head.

"Damned straight. Now let's get moving." Jones strode off, his chest puffed out.

"What's wrong?" Peter asked woozy.

"He's scared, that all." Troy answered softly. "Can you walk?" He asked, gently allowing Peter to take more and more of his own bodyweight.

"I think so. Why don't you want to go that way?" Peter asked. He looked at Troy and the expression that was reflected in the man's face blew away the haze from his mind in an instant.

"He is taking us towards the swamps. They live in the swamps." Troy shuddered as he spoke, and visibly shrank into his posture.

"What is it?"

A roar shook the trees and got both men moving. It wasn't close by, but it was enough for Peter to know they didn't want to meet what it was that had uttered the cry.

"It's worse than that, I can tell you." Troy offered, before setting off alongside Peter.

Troy knew the direction Captain Jones had been heading in, and made no rush to find him. He didn't like the man, and knew that it was highly unlikely they would survive another altercation with prisoners.

The prison world was tough, and the same gang like culture existed as it did behind the bars. "We need to be careful." Troy spoke a while later.

"Why?" Peter asked. He had regained a lot of his strength, and didn't look as pale as he had in the tree.

"We have moved into the Latino territory. Look." Troy pointed to a number of trees, which all had the same mark carved into their trunk. A cross with a long triangle that descended from the arms to a point half the crosses length below its base.

"Is that bad?" He asked

"For you and your captain, everything is bad out here. For me, yes, black guys don't go walking through the Latin ground unless you have a death wish.

"That's why you wanted to go to the plains." Peter could recall the basics of the conversation Jones and Troy had engaged in.

"Exactly. It is dangerous, but nobody has claimed it. It's open territory. We would have been safe enough there. No... I don't like being here." He was honest, and the way his eyes constantly scanned the trees, Peter understood the depth of his fear.

"Well let's keep moving. Find Captain Jones and get out of here." Peter shuddered. He could feel eyes on him. Hidden away in the trees, but the weight of their gaze was unmistakable.

Not long later they came across a patch of wet ground. The mud squelched under their feet, and the meaty aroma of fresh blood rose up.

Troy dipped his finger in the ground and gave a *tsk* when it came away red. "It's blood." He confirmed. "You still got your piece?" He asked hopeful.

"Yes." Peter said, drawing it. "But I'm still dizzy. Here, you take it." He offered the gun to Troy without thinking.

Troy paused, his hand half outstretched towards the weapon he was being offered. "You do understand that I'm in here for murder. Right?" Troy pulled his hand away. "I can't take that."

"You can and you will. I can't see straight and if it comes down to it, someone will have to shoot back. I trust you. You saved my life before you knew I was looking for you. A murderer doesn't get parole if there wasn't compelling evidence against the act." Peter pushed the gun even further towards Troy, coming close to shoving it into his chest.

Reluctantly, Troy took the gun. He held it in his hands for a few moments, before removing the safety. "Let's go." His voice was grim.

The path they had made for themselves was hard going. Heavy ferns with leaves the size of a grown man blocked their path at every step. Their stems were as thick as arms, and in some instances as wide as a human leg. It took both Troy and Peter to move one last branch out of the way before they came to a more open space. The ferns gave way to a patch of tall trees, their trunks rising so high the canopy over their heads could have been space and the thick green leaves, the night sky. In the midst of it all, knelt

Captain Jones. His face was already bloody from the fists that had been thrown at him.

A raucous cheer went up when the eyes of the group fell on Peter, his uniform giving him away. A second cheer went up when they saw the black man travelling with him.

"Looks like it's fucking Christmas." A thin and wiry looking Hispanic man spoke. The left hand side of his face was marred by a combination of tattoos scars. Signs of a tough life both sides of the bars. He smiled and his teeth were broken and cracked.

Several of the group turned on them, and someone came through the trees behind them. Strong arms shoved Peter in the back and he fell forward, collapsing onto his knees. Captain Jones gave a muffled cry, his broken lips unable to enunciate anything that came close to sounding like English. He received a knee to the ribs for his effort and was thrown to the floor.

"And you... you should know better than to wander into Latin country." The thin man addressed Troy, moving towards him with purpose. He held a stone knife in his hands.

Troy said nothing but raised the gun. He didn't point it at the man, or at any of them. Rather, he held it aloft as if he was about to start a race. The act stopped the others dead in their tracks.

"You wouldn't." The Hispanic man sneered. Thanks to his broken teeth, his voice had a slight whistle to it.

"Miguel." A worried voice spoke from the crowd.

"Try me." Troy's voice was soft and calm. He looked at Miguel, not with a start, or with any tough pretence, but simply the way one man would look at another when caught in an unfortunate situation.

None of the prisoners moved. They knew where they were, and they knew what was nearby. Jones and Peter, oblivious to the danger that lurked in the swamp got to their feet. Nobody paid them any mind.

"You get to live this time, fool. If we see you in this neighbourhood again, your ass is mine." Miguel spat, moving in close to Troy so that their noses almost touched. He gave a growl but then began to walk away.

Troy said nothing, but he stared at Miguel, his eyes starting to flicker with an intensity they had lacked before. He didn't see Jones as he moved. Diving forward, he tackled Miguel and dragged him to the floor. In a flurry of punches he drove his fists repeatedly into the man's face, only stopping when Peter grabbed him by the shoulders and managed to haul him away long enough for the others to grab their man and pull him to his feet also.

"Get off me, rookie." Jones roared, all self-control driven out of him in the final moments of his sanity. Jones threw an elbow that connected with Peter's nose. He freed himself from Peter's grip and snatched the gun from Troy's hands.

"No... don't!" Troy and most of the Latino contingency screamed in agreement. It was too late. Jones pulled the trigger and fired three shots into

Miguel's chest. Blood misted in the air and the man's small frame was thrown to the floor.

Once again, nobody moved. Their faces were pensive, etched with a fear that extended further than a man with a gun.

The growl sounded like the noise created by a jet plane flying low overhead. The ground shook as a deafening bark filled the air. A few moments later a small heard of dinosaur burst through the trees. They were no bigger than dogs, and ran on all fours. They moved fast, disappearing into the ferns in a blur of frightened squeals.

The Latino crowd also turned and ran, ignoring their fallen friend who, despite the three bullet wounds was still hopelessly clinging to life.

"You idiot." Troy snapped, snatching the gun from Jones's hands. "You just killed us all." There was no hint of humour or exaggeration in his words or in the expression etched onto his face.

"What…" Jones began, but stopped when the trunk of a tree came crashing down to the ground, falling not far from where they stood.

"That." Troy pointed at the beast that was charging towards them. It was nothing more than a shadow. A dark figure moving within the cover of the trees, but its enormity was easy enough to determine.

The creature burst through the trees, appearing to spring through into the small clearing, landing on its enormous hind legs. It fell forward, coming to rest on all fours. Its tail disappeared into the trees, making it impossible to determine its size. Not that it mattered. It was twice the size of any other creature Peter had seen, and that was all he needed to know.

The creature had a long head, its jaw easily two meters long. It hung open showing an enormous set of pointed teeth. The skin over its snout had a scarlet flare to it, while the rest of the body was a black and grey combination, stripes over the back and spots on the flank.

Its eyes found the group and its body tensed. Large nostrils flared and in an instant large spines appeared on its back. They were easily the same height as its body was, and connected by thin flaps of skin. He gave a roar that caused the air to rush over them.

"Run. Now." Troy ordered them.

"Where?" Peter called back as they ran towards the ferns.

"Anywhere." The answer was simple, but told Peter all he needed to know about the dinosaur they had woken.

The thunderous sound of its gargantuan body giving chase helped put an extra pace in Peter's strides. He ran, Troy ahead of him and Jones behind. He gave no thought to teamwork or helping his captain. All he thought about was survival.

They ran by the tree where they had hidden. The eviscerated convict was gone, a bloody smear in the ground showing the direction his body had been dragged.

The dinosaur continued to chase them, only slowed by the trees and ferns that needed to be pushed aside rather than moved around.

Running through the jungle, Peter saw light ahead of him. The trees were thinning and sunlight found the ground. The moment Peter emerged from the trees, it was blinding. They stopped with a suddenness that was bracing, and the cover of the jungle was gone in an instant. Peter's world expanded in the blink of an eye. Far above his head the sun shone in a hazy sky. The clouds were expansive but thin like a mist. They had a strange purple colouration that gave the world a delicate hue.

There was a moment which ended almost as soon as it began, where a tranquillity fell over Peter. He stood beside Troy. Both men were exhausted, sweat drenched their bodies. They stood there, surrounded by a lost world. Dinosaurs filled the open plain, herds of long necked dinosaurs and triceratops families plodded through the tall grasses. Smaller versions of the pteranodons soared overhead, and while Peter knew each of those beasts, even the gentler ones would most likely kill him in an instant, none of them seemed as terrifying as the thing that chased them.

It was precisely as his mind focused on the beast that it appeared, bursting through the trees a fraction of a second after Jones stumbled out of the wilderness.

Every creature in the vicinity looked up, and the stampede that followed saw the enormous beasts charging in every direction, except towards them, for that meant running towards the creature which may well be the devil himself.

"Run captain." Peter called out, not sure what he was urging the man to run to, for their own safety was less than guaranteed, for they still stood not more than three hundred meters from the best.

The creature had chased them on all fours, using its bulk to crash through the jungle, but now that it was in the open, it rose to his hind legs and stood taller, and more terrifying than before.

It gave a long cry and stormed towards them. Jones fell to the floor, rolling out of the way as a giant foot came close to crushing him.

Peter and Troy stood their ground. There was no cover in the plains, and the creature was faster than both of them.

"What do we do?" Peter asked.

Troy opened his mouth to talk, but the answer came out of nowhere. A second beast called out; it was a much deeper roar. Peter turned his head and the creature chasing them also altered its gaze. This was followed by a swift change of direction.

"Am I hallucinating this?" Peter asked, certain that his brain had been broken by the fever.

"Not this time." Troy answered as the Spinosaurus and the Tyrannosaurus-Rex collided.

The beasts impacted with a sound that defied description. It was two meaty trains colliding at full speed. The kind of dull heavy thud that meant only one thing… pain.

Growls and snarls echoed around the plain as the two beasts' waged war. Tails flicked and jaws snapped. A hole was torn in the flank of the Spinosaurus, and a torrent of blood flowed from the wound. A thick slab of skin and flesh flapped violently as the two continued to fight. Jaws closed around the Rex's throat, and blood began to ooze, but it shook itself free.

"Rookie, get your ass over here." Jones voice called out. Peter barely heard it above the din.

Peter and Troy turned their backs to the fight, an act harder than both wanted to admit. Jones was standing a few meter from them. His face was a swollen mess of deep purple swellings and nasty lacerations.

"What is it?" Peter asked.

"It's time." Jones answered, holding up his wrist to show them his watch. The beeping was impossible to hear above the snarling fight behind them, but the flashing red lights made it clear.

"So what happens now?" Troy asked, looking from one to the other. Jones looked from Troy to Peter and then back to Troy again. Slowly, his mangled face turned into a smile.

"Now, you're a free man my friend." Jones seemed to have resumed a modicum of his previous composure.

"How does this work?" Troy asked.

"We don't know. Not really." Peter answered. It was now Troy's turn to look from man to man, his face a picture of disbelief.

"Now we wait. We will be back home in no time." Jones spoke and then screamed as the long, thin whip-like end of the Spinosaurus tail split the earth between them.

There was a roar and a rush of wind. Peter turned and saw the jaws of the Tyrannosaurus snapping at air as its foe moved to one side. Peter threw himself to the floor and pulled Troy with him. There was a snap of teeth and then nothing but darkness.

CHAPTER 4 — SAFE AND SOUND

When Peter had arrived in the prison world, he had not been afforded the time to truly appreciate the discomfort of such a form of transportation. Returning however, was a different issue. There were no raptors waiting to eat him, and so no confusion as to his surroundings. Meaning the stomach churning nauseous waves were enjoyed in their full splendour.

Collapsing to his knees on the platform Peter vomited. While all around him people came running, shocked at the returning soldier, and his condition.

He got to his feet and saw their faces pale. His uniform was covered in blood, and his body filthy with sweat, mud, and a few tears.

A hand fell on his shoulder. Turning, Peter saw Troy, and the wide, wild look in his eyes. He was home, but his brain would not let him believe it.

"We made it?" Troy asked as the arms and hands pulled at them both, dragging them away from the stage.

Peter couldn't separate the words from the screams. *Move, get down from here. Oh my god, look at the blood.* It still didn't filter through to Peter what had happened until he and Troy had been pulled from the stage and wrapped in heat preserving blankets.

Then, turning around to face the room, Peter saw it. They had not been the only two to come through, Jones had made it. At least, most of him had. Jones upper body was lying on the transporter bed, surrounded by a sea of leaked organs and blood.

"What happened?" Peter blurted out, but the world was deaf to his query. Everybody was tending to the trauma. It was of course too late to save Jones, he was dead before he finished his journey home, but it would not do to just turn around and walk away.

Left alone, Peter and Troy looked at one another, unsure as to whether they should laugh or cry. In the end they opted for a manly hug. It allowed both the chance to hide their face while the emotion of their return ran through them.

"What the hell happened out there?" The booming voice of the warden rang out. He strode into the command center. His face was flushed and a deeper shade of red than Peter had ever seen.

The man walked with an angry stride, but Peter moved towards him. He stared at the man, and the warden stopped in his tracks.

"How many made it back?" He asked, trying to sound concerned.

"Just me." Peter spat, not offering anything more than he was asked for. "Just me, and him. Your prisoner." Peter looked over to Troy who stood alone, looking lost once more.

"What happened? It was just a simple extraction." He spat, and warm specks of his saliva peppered Peter's face.

"You know damned well what happened out there." Peter felt his anger rising.

The warden offered no response. No excuse at the ready. He tried hard to hold Peter's gaze, but was forced to lower his eyes. "You thought we would just send them away to some nice island. Do you have any idea how many prisoners this place holds, and how many more there are expected to be in the future. It's a gold mine."

"Money? These people are criminals, sure, but they are human beings, and you have them locked away down there with dinosaurs." Peter roared, and everybody slowed down to stare at him.

"Lower you voice rookie." The warned growled.

"Why, are you afraid that people will find out that you have the prisoners living in a lost prehistoric world? You don't want them knowing that the entire team got eaten by raptors or trampled by some other dinosaur." Peter was screaming at the warden whose face had deepened to an angry purple.

"That's enough. You don't know…" The warden began but Peter balled his fist and drove it into the warden's chubby face with a roar.

It was a roar that echoed around the room. It caused the windows to shake and the people to scream with alarm. It was a roar that came from outside.

Rushing towards the door, Peter and Troy shoved their way through the crowd and stood outside the control center and watched in horror as the Tyrannosaurus Rex continued to battle the Spinosaurus. Both were injured, and both were enraged. The T-Rex swung its tail and took out two of the guard huts that stood by the entrance fence to the Hard Time compound.

The two creatures took a step back from one another, and with a series of angry barks, the Spinosaurus charged at the Rex, who swung its large tail one more time. The blow caught the injured Spinosaurus across the head and sent it falling through a brick building, crushing two cars and a fence as it fell. The Tyrannosaurus leaped forward on top of its stricken foe. It would have ended the fight had a volley of automatic gun fire not attracted its attention. A group of guards had armed themselves and even as the king of the dinosaurs turned on them, they opened up a second wave. From one side, a grenade was thrown, exploding beneath the beast, adding to its rage.

Forgetting its previous fight, the Rex lowered itself, leaning forward to the point where its head was almost level with the guards. It opened its mouth with a sound that sounded like a purr, and loosed a road that had each man drop his gun and run. Stumbling over one another, the stampede of humans began, and both the Tyrannosaurus Rex and the Spinosaurus found themselves caught up in a much more one sided battle.

THE END